S0-APQ-214

The Biggest Snowball

Tika Downey

Pleasant View
Take Home Book Program

NEIGHBORHOOD READERS

Rosen Classroom Books & Materials™

New York

It started to snow.
First only a few snowflakes fell from the sky.
Then a lot of snowflakes fell from the sky.

It snowed and snowed.
It had never snowed like this before.
It just kept snowing.
There was snow everywhere.

At last it stopped snowing.
Lin and Julie met Alex and Pedro in the park.
They looked at the snow.
Snow was on everything.

"It has never snowed like this before," said Lin.
"There is so much snow!" said Alex.
"What will we do with all this snow?" asked Pedro.

"Let's make a big snowball," said Julie.
"Let's make the biggest snowball ever!" said Alex.

The children made a snowball.
It was as big as an egg.
"That's too small," said Lin.
"Let's make it bigger."

The children put on more snow.
The snowball was as big as a baseball.
"That's big," said Julie.
"But not big enough."

They put on more snow.
The snowball was as big as a basketball.
"That's big," said Pedro.
"But it's not big enough."

They kept putting on more snow.
The snowball was as big as a wheel.
Alex said, "That's still not big enough."

They put on more and more snow.
The snowball was as big as a bush.
"Let's make it bigger!" said Lin.

They put on a lot more snow.
The snowball was as big as Pedro.
"Let's make it bigger!" said Julie.

They kept putting on more snow.
The snowball was as big as a horse.
Pedro said, "That's still not big enough."

They put on more snow.
The snowball was as big as a car.
Julie said, "Let's make it even bigger!"

They kept putting on more snow.
The snowball was as big as a house.
"Now it's big enough!" said Alex.

"We've done it!" the children shouted.
"We've made the biggest snowball ever!"
"Nobody has ever made a snowball as big as ours!"